W is for Wolf

M is for Moose

S is for Salmon

B is for Bear

E is for Eagle

What is the most important thing to learn?

"What is the most important thing to learn?" I asked my teacher today. Looking puzzled she replied, "There's math, history, science, and literature... Gosh, there are so many wonderful things to learn, how can I possibly choose what is MOST important?"

Unsatisfied with such a broad answer, I decided to ask my Mom.

Mom was clearing off the dining table when I asked, "What is the most important thing to learn?" She replied without hesitation, "Treat others the way you want to be treated. If you treat people with kindness, love, and respect they are more likely to treat you the same way in return."

This seemed fair enough but I was curious what my Dad's answer might be?

Treat Others the Way you want to be treated

The Most Important Thing to Learn

WRITTEN AND ILLUSTRATED BY

TAVIA FLORENS-BOLTON

This book was created for all ages,
toddlers to teens, graduates to grandparents.
Little ones can follow along with the bold headings,
while others can appreciate the deeper message.

All rights reserved. Published by Tavia Florens-Bolton, United States of America.

ISBN 978-1-7364737-3-3

Printed in the USA

Always use your manners

I found my dad in his workshop. I asked him, "What is the most important thing to learn?" He turned off the table saw and replied, "Always use your manners. Never forget your 'pleases' and 'thank yous' and try to make eye contact when talking to someone. Manners are super cool!" he laughed.

Then in walked my uncle. I wondered what he would say about this?

Before my Dad could influence his answer, I asked my uncle, "What is the most important thing to learn?" He laughed and said, "The most important thing is to laugh. Laugh everyday. It's good for the heart, mind, and soul. Laughing can even relieve stress!"

I smiled. "Smile and the world will smile back at you," he said.

"This seemed like pretty silly advice, but maybe there was something to it," I thought. I wondered what my aunt would say about this?

LAUGH

JUNE

21
Summer
Solstice

MANAGE YOUR TIME

I called up my aunt and asked her, "What is the most important thing to learn?"
She thought briefly before saying, "Manage your time, prioritize, and multi-task.
Have self-discipline and don't procrastinate."

"Everyone has such different answers," I thought.
"I think I'll go ask my neighbor!"

My neighbor was tidying up her kitchen when I asked her,
"What is the most important thing to learn?"
As she poured her coffee she replied, "Be dependable. Do
what you say you are going to do and always be on time."

Just then we heard a knock on the door. It was the mailman.
"Oh," I thought as I ran to the entryway.
"Maybe I can ask him!"

DON'T FORGET RIGHT FROM WRONG

RIGHT   WRONG

I knew the mailman
was in a hurry so I asked
him quickly, "What's the most
important thing to learn?"
He handed us the mail and swiftly
replied, "Don't forget right from wrong!
It won't be easy, but always
listen to your gut. Be honest
and trustworthy."

"Thank you!" I shouted.
As he walked away I spotted my
Grandma's car in my driveway.
I wondered what she would say?

Make your own path

"Hi Grandma! What is the most important thing to learn?" I asked. She hugged me and said, "Make your own path. Don't compare yourself to others. Be proud of yourself and your accomplishments. I bet your grandpa would have a wise answer. He should be here any minute!"

I was excited to hear what my grandpa would have to say!

Hard work pays off

Before I knew it my Grandpa walked into the room.
"What is the most important thing to learn?" I asked him.
He hung his cane on the back of his chair and said, "Hard work pays off.
Work first, play later. You have to balance work and play, because you
need both. Choose a career that complements the life you want to live."

My Grandpa is a smart man, so I need to remember this.
As I pondered his advice he asked, "Have you asked your sister?"

LOVE YOURSELF

Ask my sister? Why would I do that? She is younger than me.
What could I possibly learn from a four year old?
But my Grandpa is a smart man, so I decided to give it a try.

"What is the most important thing to learn?" I asked my sister.
In her little voice she replied, "To love you."
My grandpa leaned over to me and added, "It's important to
love and value yourself. Embrace what makes you unique."

"Wow," I thought, "maybe I should go ask my cousin too!"

Be kind

My cousin was getting ready
for his soccer game when
I asked, "What is the most
important thing to learn?"
He grinned and said, "To be kind.
Kindness can carry you with grace
through a tough situation. It takes
less energy to be kind than it
does to be unkind."
"Very sweet," I thought.

We were headed to the library
that afternoon, So I made sure
to ask the librarian.

Don't let technology get in your way

As I wandered around looking for a book,
I found the librarian and asked,
"What is the most important thing to learn?"
She tipped her glasses down and in a sweet
voice replied, "Don't let technology get in
your way. Get out in nature.
Go hang out with people. Lift your eyes
up from the screen to talk to someone.
Last but certainly not least,
read books - actual paper books."

I love to read so I started looking
for a book to check out, when
my friend from school and
her mother walked over.

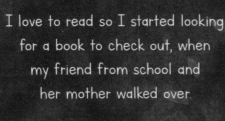

SET GOALS

I asked my friend's mother, "What is the most important thing to learn?"
She proudly replied, "The most important thing to learn is how to set goals.
How to take personal responsibility for your dreams. You can do hard things,
you just need to take action and feel the momentum grow."
"That's very rewarding," I thought.

After checking out my books, it was time to go out for dinner.
I wondered what the waitress would tell me.

Take care of your body, mind, and soul

After the waitress took our order, I asked her,
"What is the most important thing to learn?"
As she collected our menus she replied, "Take care of
your body, mind, and soul. Exercise is power. Eat well,
wash your hands, and make time for quiet."

"Interesting," I thought, "my doctor once told me that
I only get one body so I need to take care of it!"
Say, I should ask my doctor!

Never give up

Today was my day for check ups. When my doctor came into the
room I asked her, "What is the most important thing to learn?"
"That's an excellent question!" she said as she washed her hands.
"I think the most important thing to learn is to never give up!
You are going to fail at times. Believe in yourself and keep
trying until you meet your goal."
"Thank you doc!" I said.

Next I was headed to the dentist.
I couldn't wait to hear what he would say!

While we sat in the dentist's waiting room, I decided to ask the receptionist, "What is the most important thing to learn?"

STAND TALL

She looked up from her computer and replied, "Stand tall. Do what makes you happy. Stand up for what you believe in and always vote."

As I began to think of what career would make me happy, in happened to walk my mom's best friend for her dentist appointment.

After checking in for her appointment, my mom's best friend sat next to me.
"What is the most important thing to learn?" I asked her.
She kindly replied, "Choose your friends wisely. Value your friendships and be a
good friend. You deserve love and respect in return. Surround yourself with
positive people because the people in your life help mold who you are."
She and my mom have been best friends for years, so I value this advice greatly.

"Excuse me," the receptionist said. "the dentist is ready to see you now."

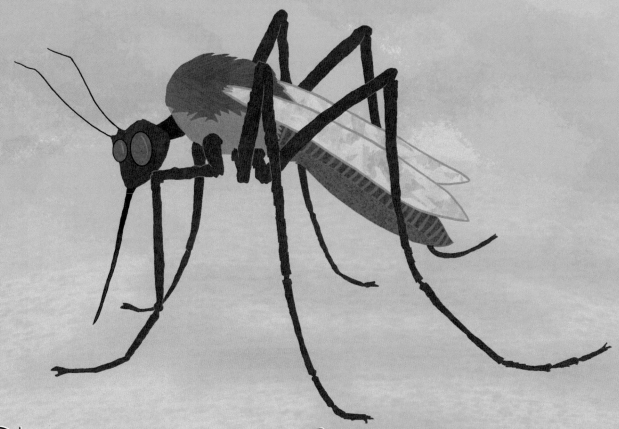

Choose your friends wisely

IT WILL PASS

As I sat down in the exam chair I asked the dentist, "What is the most important thing to learn?"
He chuckled and said, "That it will pass. Tough times get easier, things change, and time heals. You have the strength to handle what has been given to you."

I didn't really understand what he was talking about so I decided I would ask my coach later at practice.

CHEER FOR OTHERS

At practice I asked my coach,
"What is the most important thing to learn?"
As she turned on the music she replied,
"Cheer for others and celebrate their success.
Learn to be as happy for other people's gifts,
joy, and wealth as you are for your own."

"That seems easy enough," I thought.
I think tomorrow morning I'll ask my bus driver.

As I boarded the school bus I asked my bus driver,
"What is the most important thing to learn?"
He peacefully replied, "To be patient. Sleep on your ideas.
Good things come to those who wait."
"Thank you," I said as I found an open seat.

Later at gym class, I think I'll ask my gym teacher.

BE PATIENT

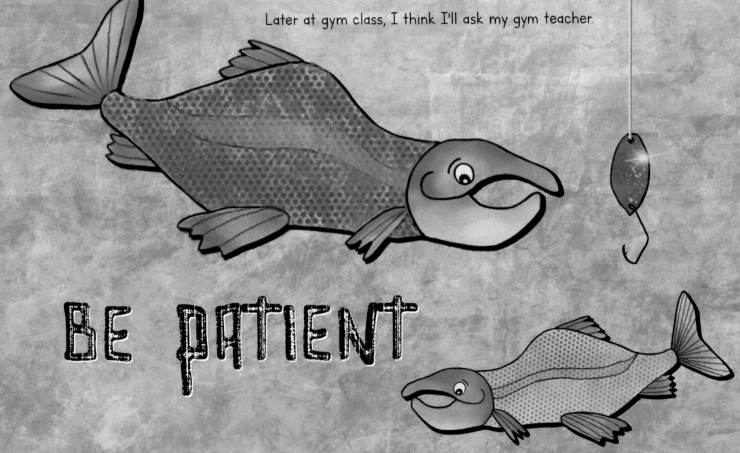

TRY SOMETHING NEW

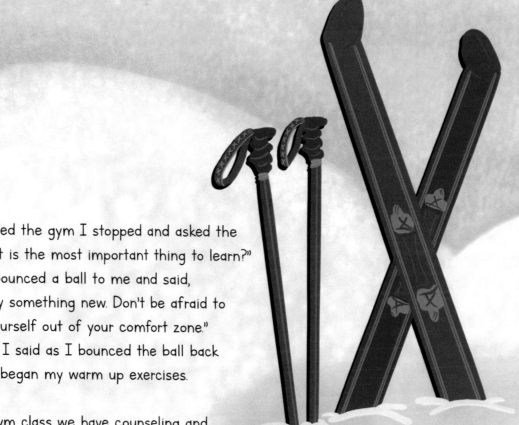

As we entered the gym I stopped and asked the
teacher, "What is the most important thing to learn?"
He bounced a ball to me and said,
"Always try something new. Don't be afraid to
push yourself out of your comfort zone."
"Thanks!" I said as I bounced the ball back
and began my warm up exercises.

After gym class we have counseling and
my counselor always has great advice.

Tomorrow is a new day

As we walked into the counselor's room I asked her, "What is the most important thing to learn?"
In a soft voice she replied, "That tomorrow is a new day. It's a fresh start, a chance to start over,
and a chance to do better."

A few moments later the principal came in to deliver a message.
I wonder what her answer will be?

you don't know everything

I walked across the room and in a low voice I
asked the principal, "What do you think is the
most important thing to learn?"
She thoughtfully replied, "You know a lot, but you
don't know everything. Be open to new ideas and
opinions. Experience makes you stronger and wiser.
Let others help you and never stop learning."
"Interesting," I thought.

After school I have my piano lesson
so I can ask my piano teacher.

Be cReaTive

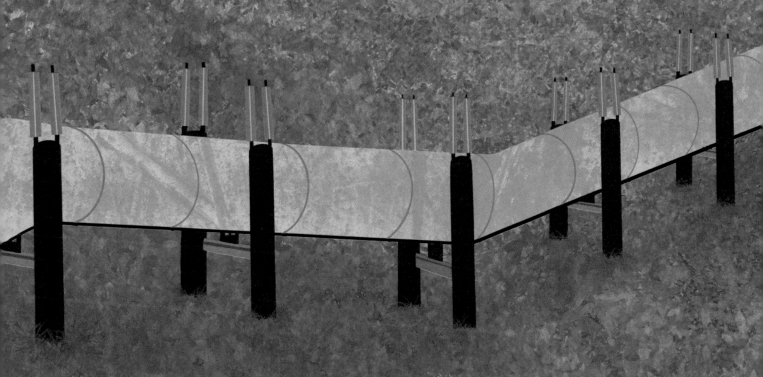

Before my piano lesson began I asked my piano teacher,
"What is the most important thing to learn?"
As she straightened my sheet music she replied,
"The most important thing to learn is how to be creative.
Use your imagination and your talents. Always seek inspiration
and exercise both sides of your brain. Music is a wonderful
way to express yourself and your creativity!"
"That's a wonderful answer," I thought.

After my lesson we will be stopping by the farmer's market to
pick up some vegetables. My dad's friend is a local farmer who
sells his produce at the market. I wonder what he would say?

MAKE THE WORLD A BETTER PLACE

At the market we found my dad's farmer friend, so I ran up to his booth and asked him, "What is the most important thing to learn?"
Looking very pleased he replied, "Make the world a better place. Help others, be generous, have empathy, and always smile at those around you. Clean up after yourself and leave places better than you found them. Be the change you want to see."
"That is very powerful," I thought.

Tomorrow our class is taking a field trip to the fire department.
I bet I could ask a firefighter!

On a tour of the fire station, I asked one of the firefighters,
"What is the most important thing to learn?"
He beamed and replied, "Be a giver, volunteer, and always pay it forward.
Give and you shall receive. Find ways to fill someone's bucket of happiness."
"That's so nice," I thought.

After school my dog had a check-up, so I thought I'd ask the vet.

pay it forward

After the vet listened to my dog's heart I asked,
"What is the most important thing to learn?"
"Be thankful," she said. "Show gratitude
and write thank you notes. Focus on
the wonderful things you have
instead of what you don't have."
I could see this was very valuable.

As we were leaving, a state
trooper canine unit was parked
outside. I was very interested in
what the trooper would say!

Be thankful

PAY ATTENTION TO THE WORLD AROUND YOU

The trooper was loading his German Shepherd dog into his vehicle when I decided to ask, "What is the most important thing to learn?" He shut the door and knelt down to respond, "Pay attention to the world around you. Enjoy the many sights to see but be aware of your surroundings. Learn about both the good and the bad. Remember that most stories have at least two perspectives."

This one will take some practice I realized.

The next day, I had camp and I knew there would be someone to ask there.

We started the camp day off at the pool. After we did some water activities, I asked the life guard, "What is the most important thing to learn?" He calmly replied, "The most important thing to learn is how to relax. Find what calms you. Get eight hours of sleep each night, meditate, breathe, pray, and be present."

Relax

This is very smart advice.

After we finished our camp activities, I asked my camp counselor what she thought

Explore

"What is the most important thing to learn?"
I asked my camp leader. As she tied her hiking boots,
she looked up at me and replied, "You must get out and explore!
There is so much to learn from places you haven't been.
Get outside, seek adventure, and go somewhere new.
You will never regret prioritizing experiences over
material things." I wondered what she meant by that?

After camp we went by the store.
I hesitated but then decided to ask the store clerk.

YOU AREN'T ALWAYS RIGHT

"What is the most important thing to learn?"
I asked the store clerk. He paused while
scanning our groceries and replied, "It is important to
learn that you aren't always right. Everyone makes
mistakes and you will make mistakes too.
Learn from your mistakes and move on.
Winning and losing are just part of life."

"Refreshing insight," I thought.

After we loaded up the groceries, we were
headed over to my great grandparents'
house for a big family dinner.
I wondered what they would say?

Live within your means

When we arrived I asked my great grandmother,
"What is the most important thing to learn?"
She hugged me and said, "The most important thing is to live within your means.
Be humble. Save, budget, and shop smart. Purchase mindfully, not everything
you buy needs to be new. The things you buy need to be maintained, cleaned,
moved, and stored. Don't give these items too much of your time, as over
time they will just gather dust. Simple is better and less is more."

"Thank you!" I replied. Then I asked my great grandfather.

However, before I could ask my question, my great grandfather asked me,
"What do YOU think is the most important thing to learn?"
I paused for a moment to reflect on everyone's answers only to realize that they were all equally important. With that I replied, "The most important thing to learn is that it takes a village. It takes family, friends, as well as an entire community to learn from. You should help and support each other in all that you do. There is something to learn from everyone you meet."

My great grandfather smiled, "I couldn't have said it better myself."

IT TAKES A VILLAGE